Mum says she'll be back very soon.

She'll pick us up when she's done her shopping.

Let's play with the water
first, Bear.

Now I'll paint a picture.
This is much too messy
for you, Bear!

This is fun!

At storytime, I'm so thirsty
I have three drinks!

Then we all rush around...

except Dotty, she's too tired.

When Mum comes to
pick us up, I tell her
we've been fine!